Dear Parent:

Rhythm and rhyme make language come alive. Words become fun and funny. Couple those words with pictures that add sparkle and whimsy, and the result is a picture book that makes children and adults giggle with delight.

While it looks like pure fun, *Sheep in a Shop* is a fine example of the power of expression. In this book, children **hear** the way combinations of words can sound; they **see** how line drawings and even colors evoke a variety of feelings.

This is the second *Sheep* book we have shared with our members. (You may remember *Sheep in a Jeep*.) This new book has already been selected as one of the year's best books, and we hope you and your child enjoy it too.

Sincerely,

Stephen Fraser

Stephen Fraser
Senior Editor
Weekly Reader Books

Sheep in a Shop

Weekly Reader Children's Book Club Presents

Sheep in a Shop

Nancy Shaw
Illustrated by Margot Apple

Houghton Mifflin Company Boston

Also by Nancy Shaw and illustrated by Margot Apple:

Sheep in a Jeep
Sheep on a Ship

This book is a presentation of Newfield
Publications, Inc. Newfield Publications offers
book clubs for children from preschool through
high school. For further information write to:
Newfield Publications, Inc., 4343 Equity Drive,
Columbus, Ohio 43228.

Published by arrangement with Houghton Mifflin
Company. Newfield Publications is a trademark
of Newfield Publications, Inc. Weekly Reader
is a federally registered trademark of Weekly
Reader Corporation.

Library of Congress Cataloging-in-Publication Data

Shaw, Nancy (Nancy E.)
    Sheep in a Shop / Nancy Shaw; illustrated by Margot Apple.
        p.   cm.
    Summary: Sheep hunt for a birthday present and make havoc of the
shop, only to discover they haven't the money to pay for things.
    ISBN 0-395-53681-2
    [1. Sheep – Fiction.   2. Shopping – Fiction.   3. Stories in rhyme.]
I. Apple, Margot, ill.   II. Title.
PZ8.3.S5334Shm   1991   90-4139
[E] – dc20   CIP
                               AC

Printed in the United States of America

WOZ 10   9   8   7   6   5   4   3

To Fred, for suggesting a birthday theme, to Scott, for
sharing many happy birthdays, and to my parents, for making
birthdays possible.

—N.S.

For these sheep-loving shopkeepers: Anne; Barbara & Art;
Claire, David & Diana; Cree, Ann & Marcia; Jan; Janet;
Leslie & Maude; Linda; Mark; Michael; Nancy.

—M.A.

A birthday's coming! Hip hooray!

Five sheep shop for the big, big day.

Sheep find rackets. Sheep find rockets.

Sheep find jackets full of pockets.

Sheep find blocks.

Sheep wind clocks.

Sheep try trains. Sheep fly planes.

Sheep decide to buy a beach ball.

Sheep prefer an out-of-reach ball.

Sheep climb. Sheep grumble.

Sheep reach. Sheep fumble.

Sheep sprawl.

Boxes tumble.

Boxes fall in one big jumble.

Sheep put back the beach ball stack.

They choose some ribbon

from the rack.

They dump their bank. Pennies clank.

There's not enough to buy this stuff.

Sheep blink. Sheep think.

What can they swap to pay the shop?

Sheep clip wool, three bags full.

Sheep trade.

The bill is paid.

Sheep hop home in the warm spring sun.

They're ready for some birthday fun.